IVAN ZHUK: ZHUK'S G[
THE MMA FIG]
by
Maxwell Hoffn.

Ivan Zhuk: Zhuk's Gambit Book 2 The MMA Fighter

Ivan Zhuk: Zhuk's Gambit, Volume 2

Maxwell Hoffman

Published by Maxwell Hoffman, 2024.

This is a work of fiction. Similarities to real people, places, or events are entirely coincidental.

IVAN ZHUK: ZHUK'S GAMBIT BOOK 2 THE MMA FIGHTER

First edition. October 20, 2024.

Copyright © 2024 Maxwell Hoffman.

ISBN: 979-8227862747

Written by Maxwell Hoffman.

Also by Maxwell Hoffman

Benny Dubious Playbook Scheme Series 3
Benny Dubious Playbook Scheme Trouble in Georgia: The Moshie Affair
Benny Dubious Playbook Scheme Trouble in Georgia Book 2: "Moshie's" Fall
Benny Dubious Playbook Scheme Trouble in Georgia Book 3: Hugo's Revelation

Ivan Zhuk: Zhuk's Gambit
Ivan Zhuk: Zhuk's Gambit Book 1 Mental Agony
Ivan Zhuk: Zhuk's Gambit Book 2 The MMA Fighter

Misadventures of Wolfgang Wirrarr
Misadventures of Wolfgang Wirrarr Omnibus Trilogy

Rowan Sunfire Frosty Fugitive Series
Rowan Sunfire Frosty Fugitive Book 3 Defense of Vos Tower
Rowan Sunfire Frosty Fugitive Omnibus Trilogy

Watch for more at https://www.instagram.com/vader7800/.

Table of Contents

Part One 1
Prologue 2
Chapter One 10
Chapter Two 18
Chapter Three 26
Part Two 33
Chapter Four 34
Chapter Five 43
Chapter Six 52
Chapter Seven 60
Part Three 67
Chapter Eight 68
Chapter Nine 76
Chapter Ten 83
Epilogue 91

Part One

Prologue

The Truce

#

Yuri Kozlov, Tamrat Hailu and Emnet Tasia all found themselves in the media area of the prison. The medics were doing their best trying to give them pain medication for the burns that they had received from the boiling water that was poured on by Ivan Zhuk.

#

"I can't believe he did that" said Emnet.

#

Emnet was just laughing along with the others with the jokes by Yuri and Tamrat. It was a tag team affair. Yuri gazed at Tamrat as he tried to get up, the burns were all over his face.

#

"I am sorry that I had caused so much trouble to you in the past" said Yuri.

#

"We all make mistakes" said Tamrat, "you thought you could control the prison better than I did."

#

"But we all can agree that Ivan Zhuk is trouble" continued Yuri.

#

The two Ethiopians nodded to the lone Russian national.

#

"Yea, it seems that way" sighed Tamrat, "I thought I could use him to take back the prison."

#

"And look where it ended up all of us" added Yuri.

#

"We should have a truce" suggested Emnet.

#

A truce, what choice did Tamrat have in his condition? He was already getting annoyed with Ivan's unpredictable behavior. The three prisoners agreed to a temporary truce once they were allowed to go back to the rest of the prison population.

#

Ivan in Mental Agony

#

While Yuri, Tamrat and Emnet made an unlikely pact, Ivan Zhuk was still sitting in his solitary confinement cell. His conscious ghost version of Ms. Angelica Esposito was present trying to comfort him.

#

"You must be regretting pouring the boiling water on those men" said Angelica.

\#

Ivan gazed up at the conscious ghost.

\#

"Yes, I do feel like I did something terrible to them" sighed Ivan.

\#

Ivan couldn't believe this was transpiring so fast. He remembered the wise words of Enrico Russo. He knew he would be disappointed with this brand of behavior of his.

\#

"I just cannot believe I still did it" said Ivan.

\#

Ivan had so much sorrow for what he did, but knew he would have to face the consequences. As the hours ticked by, Enrico Russo who was in his cell went about the usual activities of the prison. From the roll call to eating at the mess hall. There was fear among the prisoners over Ivan's own behavior. Enrico could observe the prisoners as he ate at his table by himself at the mess hall.

\#

"That guy has problems" remarked one Hispanic prisoner.

\#

"I agree" said a white prisoner, "he has done grave harm to three top bosses of the prison."

#

"He's a threat to all of us" added a black gang member.

#

There was an agreement with the prison population on Ivan, and Enrico knew he had to come to his defense.

#

Shocked Boris

#

Ivan's actions also had a ripple effect even from the outside of the prison. Boris Orlova in particular was outraged by the most recent episode. The warden had one of his representatives call Boris over the incident since he knew Boris was trying to get Ivan free.

#

"HE DID WHAT?!" cried Boris as he was on his cellphone with the representative.

#

"He poured boiling water on three men who were making fun of him" said the representative, "the warden told me this, as statements from various prison guards."

#

Boris nearly wanted to throw his phone on the ground over this incident. Ivan Zhuk was sabotaging his own chances of freedom!

\#

"I can't believe I t, he's doing this to himself!" cried Boris.

\#

Boris' yelling on the phone could be hear throughout the mansion, particularly reaching the ears of Vikor Zhuk, Ivan's brother. Viktor headed over to the source of the noise, he could see Boris was upset over what Ivan did in prison.

\#

"THAT IDIOT IS RUINING HIS OWN CHANCES!" cried Boris.

\#

Boris ended the phone call and noticed Viktor was present just for a little bit of the conversation.

\#

Viktor in Disbelief

\#

Viktor had so much disbelief in himself as he gazed at Boris.

\#

"What happened, what did my brother do?" asked Viktor.

\#

"He poured boiling water on men who were making fun of him when he was manning the kitchen area" continued Boris, "your brother is ruining his chances of freedom."

#

Boris knew he had to contact the attorney who agreed to help with Ivan's case. That would be the next step, he would probably have to hire some security in the prison to make sure Ivan wouldn't get into anymore trouble. The Italian mobster Enrico wouldn't be enough to help with the matter.

#

"I have to speak to the attorney" sighed Boris.

#

Boris began to dial Ms. Angelica's number on his cellphone, she picked up immediately.

#

"Boris, how are things going?" asked Angelica.

#

This was the real attorney for Ivan's case, not the conscious version going around trying to help Ivan. Boris had to repeat the terrible story from prison to the attorney, her mouth dropped on the other end.

#

"He did what?!" cried Angelica.

#

"He poured boiling water on men in the prison, he is ruining your chances" continued Boris.

#

"I will have another meeting with him—" said Angelica.

#

"No, we need to make sure someone needs to be in the prison with him and it can't be another prisoner" continued Boris.

#

Boris would need to find someone who would help protect Ivan and keep him out of trouble. But who thought Boris.

Chapter One

<u>Turning to an MMA Fighter</u>

#

Boris had little options left on the table after hearing about Ivan's most recent incident in prison. He checked out certain profiles of MMA fighters and one stood out - Daniel Ward a former Major within the military and a veteran of the Iraq War. He headed over towards Olga's room.

#

"I need you to do some research on Major Daniel Ward" said Boris.

#

"Checking" said Olga.

#

Olga gazed at the profile from her father's smart phone and began to bring up the profile on her laptop. She was rather fast at her research.

#

"So what do you want to do with him?" asked Olga as she pulled up the profile.

#

"I need him to make sure Ivan Zhuk stays out of trouble in prison, I got a sense that the prisoners he poured boiling water on him will go after him and anyone who defends him" continued Boris.

#

Boris had every right to be worried for Ivan's safety, time was ticking away and Ivan's time in solitary confinement would soon be over. Olga managed to pull up the contact information of Daniel Ward.

#

"Daniel Ward, mixed race male, apparently his mother was black and his father was white" said Olga.

#

"Forward me his contact information" said Boris.

#

Olga soon sent the phone number and email address of Daniel Ward. Boris had high hopes he would be reaching the former Major soon.

#

Contacting Major Daniel Ward

#

Boris was desperate trying to get answers, he knew the former Major would be interested in Ivan's case. As he called the Major's number, Daniel picked up on the other end.

#

"Yes, this is former Major Daniel Ward speaking sir!" said Daniel on the other end.

#

"Major, I need your help, I am Boris Orlova, the anti-government Russian national known for arms deals with Ukraine" said Boris, "I need your assistance in protecting a client of mine in prison."

#

The former Major listened in on Boris' every word.

#

"I understand, this Ivan Zhuk sounds like he could explode at any moment" said Daniel.

#

"And we need you to get into the prison and protect him" continued Boris.

#

"But I have never been charged with anything" added Daniel.

#

"I understand, which is the reason why you will be working as a prison guard my daughter will hack into their system and you will sign up for that job" said Boris.

#

"Don't you worry, I will not fail you" said Daniel.

#

Olga sighed as she knew she had her work cut out. It wasn't hard for her to hack into the prison system and create a job application for the former Major to sign up.

#

The Fake Prison Guard

#

Within moments, the job application appeared in the former Major's in box.

#

"Ah yes, looks official" said Daniel.

#

Daniel soon enters in his information and hits submit, he knew within days he would be hired. With his skills as an MMA fighter would be no problem handling the other prisoners aside from Ivan. He could only hope he wouldn't be too late. For Ivan Zhuk, he was soon to be released back into the prison population.

#

"Come on Ivan, you're solitary confinement time is over" said the prison guard.

#

Ivan soon was brought out in chains, he gazed around the various occupied cells. All the prisoners feared Ivan for pouring the boiling water on Yuri, Tamrat and Emnet the other day.

#

"He frightens me!" cried a white male prisoner.

#

"Keep him away!" added a black gang member.

#

The frighten prisoners didn't know what Ivan would do next. Except for Enrico Russo who felt he could still get through to Ivan.

#

"Ivan, I know you're in there somewhere thinking about what you did" said Enrico, "I can still help you if you just give me a chance."

#

Ivan had a nasty glance towards Enrico, and the Italian mobster backed off.

#

"Okay, okay" said Enrico, "I get it, I get it."

#

The Italian mobster felt it was best to leave Ivan alone. As Ivan was led into his cell, it would soon be the former Major's turn to come face to face with Ivan Zhuk.

#

The New Prison Guard

#

The former Major Daniel Ward got good news that he received the job offer instantly for the prison where Ivan Zhuk was staying. He couldn't believe it was that fast. He arrived a few days to the prison for his first day on the job. As he drove in, he headed towards the check in.

#

"You must be the new prison guard everyone has been talking about" said one of the prison guards at the check in, "the warden will show you around after you get dressed in uniform."

#

There was no traditional job interview for prison guards, their skills alone would match up with the job. The former Major despite being overqualified was welcomed instantly. As he headed towards the locker, Daniel put on the uniform and sent a text message to Boris.

#

"I am in" said Daniel in the text message.

#

"Good" said Boris, "when you are on duty keep a look out for Ivan."

#

"Will do" said Daniel.

#

Daniel headed off and soon greeted the warden.

#

"Ah yes, former Major Daniel Ward" said the warden as he greeted him with a military salute, "so glad that you joined our prison family. Though I am surprised there was a job application open for prison guard."

#

"Well, it was by luck I came across it" said Daniel.

#

The warden then gave Daniel the tour of the prison.

Chapter Two

Touring the Prison Montage

\#

The tour by the warden was pretty fast - it ranged from the hallways that Daniel would have to patrol, the mess hall, the exercise and free time areas. And also the chores which the prisoners were asked to do around the prison.

\#

"This is your day to day operation former Major" said the warden, "you are to observe everything the prisoners do and report any issues to your ranking official."

\#

"Can do" said Daniel.

\#

Daniel continued to listen in on the warden's every word, after the tour was finished Daniel was soon shown where Ivan Zhuk's cell was located.

\#

"This is the cell of the notorious Ivan Zhuk" said the warden, "he's not in his cell at the moment since he's doing chores around the prison. But this is where he would be."

\#

Daniel took a peak inside the cell, nothing special about Ivan's cell.

\#

"The prisoners, are they afraid of him?" asked Daniel.

\#

"Well there was an incident a few days ago where he threw boiling water on some other prisoners" said the warden, "they will be out from the medical area of our prison very soon."

\#

The warden soon said his goodbye to Daniel, and Daniel decided to stick around Ivan's cell.

\#

Keeping a Watchful Eye

\#

Daniel strolled around the surrounding cells near Ivan's. He could tell that the prisoners will still out.

\#

"That troublemaker sure brings so much fear here" said Daniel in his head.

\#

The former Major knew he had similar troublemakers in his unit like Ivan and felt he could handle the Ukrainian national. He soon heard it was dinner time for the prisoners and decided to stroll towards the mess hall with the other guards. Much to everyone's surprise, Ivan had an entire table to himself. The black gang members loyal to Tamrat and Emnet sat at their own table with Yuri's loyalists sitting at another. Enrico Russo sat at the far end of a table that Ivan was eating at.

#

"What happened back there?" whispered Enrico.

#

Ivan refused to speak to Enrico as he ate his dinner. He couldn't believe everyone was frighten of him. It was just like how it was back during the immigration center against the other immigrants.

#

"You must be so lonely eating by yourself" continued Enrico.

#

"Don't come close to me" said Ivan.

#

There was much fear in the mess hall, Daniel could notice the shift as he headed inside.

#

Finally Meeting Ivan

#

Daniel gazed at Ivan, this was the man who caused so much of the commotion in prison? The former Major knew he had to approach Ivan with caution. He didn't want to cause any further issues with the Ukrainian.

#

"Why are you looking at me?" asked Ivan as he gazed at Daniel.

#

"Uh, I am a new guard, I was just hired today" said Daniel.

#

Ivan felt something was off with this new prison guard. He got some sort of sense he had run-ins with people similar like him.

#

"Please be careful around him" whispered one of Yuri's henchmen, "he poured boiling water on our boss the other day. We all saw it."

#

The other prisoners despite their differences all agreed on fearing Ivan's presence. Daniel would have to convince the prisoners that he could get Ivan out and things would go back to normal. But the mess hall wouldn't be the right area to say it. Ivan continued to eat his meal and got up without taking the tray to the kitchen counter.

#

"Well that's just rude" thought Daniel in his head.

#

Daniel ended up picking up Ivan's tray, however that soon triggered Ivan.

#

Triggered Ivan

#

Ivan was already offended with all of the teasing and the mockery coming from the fellow prisoners. He glanced over at the new prison guard.

#

"YOU PUT MY TRAY DOWN!" bellowed Ivan.

#

"I am just trying to clean up after you" said Daniel.

#

Daniel tried to be calm, he didn't want to reveal too much about himself or show off his MMA fighting skills, at least not yet. There was a tense moment in the mess hall, all of the prisoners knew the new prison guard screwed up on his first day.

#

"Now you're going to get it" said a black gang member as he rolled his eyes.

#

Ivan began to take a few steps towards Daniel.

#

"PUT MY TRAY BACK" said Ivan.

#

"You mean to the kitchen counter?" asked Daniel.

#

"NO, THE TABLE!" bellowed Ivan.

#

Ivan was enraged over something so small and little that was setting him off. Enrico knew he had to step in and be the brave one.

#

"ENOUGH!" cried Enrico.

#

Enrico surprised everyone by standing in between Ivan and Daniel. He didn't want Ivan to hurt anyone else.

#

"Ivan, I care about you as a fellow prisoner, you know this will only hurt you more if you go any further" said Enrico.

#

The Italian mobster was doing his best trying to show some humanity, but Ivan wasn't listening at all.

Chapter Three

<u>Ivan Lunges!</u>

\#

Ivan had enough of Enrico's disruptions to his daily life in the prison. He began to tackle as he lunged towards the Italian mobster. The other prisoners froze in fear from all sides at the fight of Ivan's brutal behavior. Daniel had no choice but to break up the fight.

\#

"ENOUGH!" cried Daniel.

\#

Daniel with one punch sent Ivan tumbling to the floor, it was enough to knock Ivan unconscious. Enrico glanced over the unconscious Ivan.

\#

"Who are you?" asked Enrico.

\#

The other prisoners oddly began to cheer on the new prison guard as a celebrity!

\#

"Say, what's your name you guard?" asked a black gang member.

\#

"Former Major Daniel Ward" said Daniel.

\#

"Well Daniel, you made sure that troublemaker wouldn't cause anymore fights" said the black gang member.

\#

The medics soon arrived and placed Ivan on a stretcher. Daniel didn't know if he had screwed up his job in protecting Ivan. He was just doing his job as a prison guard trying to protect other prisoners. For Ivan, he was soon taken to another wing of the medical area far from where Yuri, Tamrat and Emnet were. The trio were on the verge of recovery when they noticed Ivan on a stretcher.

\#

Who Knocked Out Ivan?

\#

The medics at the medical area of the prison told Yuri, Tamrat and Emnet that they could head back into the prison population the following morning. They glanced over Ivan's unconscious body as he was taken to a separate area of the media area of the prison.

\#

"What, someone did our job for us?!" cried Tamrat.

\#

Tamrat had a crackle over this, he couldn't believe Ivan got himself into trouble again.

"That fool thinks he could do whatever he wants in prison" said Emnet.

#

"I wonder who was responsible for knocking him out" said Yuri, "I wish it was one of us to have done it."

#

"Well, we'll find out tomorrow morning" said Tamrat, "we are scheduled to go back into the prison population."

#

For poor Ivan, the conscious ghost of Ms. Angelica Esposito hovered over his body. She knew Ivan was still alive but his actions had consequences to his behavior. About an hour later, Ivan wakes up finding himself in the hospital area.

#

"What happened?!" cried Ivan.

#

"You were punched in the face for daring to lunge at Enrico" said Angelica, "you know he was one of your committed supporters in prison."

Ivan felt terrible, he couldn't believe the new prison guard had triggered him to do something like that.

#

Checking on Ivan

#

The medics at the medical area of the prison soon headed over towards Ivan's bed once he was awake.

#

"Good, you're up, that concussion you received didn't kill you at all" said a medic.

#

"I can't believe someone got the upper hand" said Ivan.

#

"You shouldn't have gotten into another fight" added a second medic.

#

The conscious ghost of Angelica was floating around Ivan in agreement with the medics.

#

"See, you should have never fought Enrico like that, the new guard was just protecting him and trying to be polite to take your tray back to the kitchen counter" said Angelica.

Ivan still felt so bad and terrible, he knew it would be sometime before he would be released. For Enrico, he was safe and sound in his cell. He gazed over and noticed the new prison guard on patrol.

#

"Say, I would like to say thank you again for coming to my defense" said Enrico.

#

"It was nothing, it's in the job description" said Daniel.

#

"The name is Enrico Russo, I use to run the Italian mafia in Chicago" said Enrico, "but sadly our days have been numbered with new criminal enterprises taking over our businesses."

#

"You defended that Ivan Zhuk?" asked Daniel.

#

"Yea, I tried to show him the ropes of the prison, he refused" continued Enrico.

#

"Do tell" continued Daniel.

Chatting Away

\#

Both Enrico and Daniel got to know each other on a more personal level. Since Daniel came to Enrico's rescue on punching Ivan's lights out.

\#

"So you fought in the Iraq War?" asked Enrico.

\#

"It was very brutal" said Daniel, "I know I was serving my country, but it was too much for me."

\#

"Yea, I can imagine" added Enrico, "being a veteran of a war like that would drive anyone crazy."

\#

Daniel didn't tell Enrico he was working for Boris, though both men had met Boris before.

\#

"You're also an MMA fighter, no wonder you were able to easily defeat Ivan" laughed Enrico.

\#

"Yep" said Daniel, "practice makes perfect with every fight I get into. Sadly for Ivan he needs to learn his lesson not to cause any further trouble."

#

As the conversation continued between them, the other prisoners soon heard familiar voices coming down the hallways. The prison guards were escorting Yuri Kozlov, Tamrat Hailu and Emnet Tasifa back to their cells. They had since healed from their injuries.

#

"Glad to see you back boss" said a black gang member to Tamrat.

#

"Welcome back boss" said one of Yuri's henchmen.

#

Yuri, Tamrat and Emnet greeted the prisoners as they soon arrived in their cells. But the trio caught the attention of a new guard who was speaking to Enrico as they were all arriving back.

Part Two

Chapter Four

New Guard?

\#

Yuri could see the new guard was being rather chatty with Enrico Russo in his cell.

\#

"You are seeing what I am seeing?" asked Yuri to the other prisoners.

\#

"Hey show some respect to the new guard he's a former Major and an MMA fighter" added one of the white male prisoners.

\#

"Yea, he saved Enrico's life from Ivan the other day" added a male Hispanic prisoner.

\#

Yuri was intrigued over the new guard and so were Tamrat and Emnet.

\#

"This could put a damper on our plans if we are to go after Ivan" said Tamrat.

\#

"Nonsense, he just needs some sort of distraction" said Yuri, "then either one of us can handle Ivan alone."

\#

"Wait, you want me to provide the distraction?" asked Emnet.

\#

"Well, you are a rank lower than me in my own gang so you will have to do" said Tamrat.

\#

Emnet groaned, he hated being friendly with the prison guards in general. But this particular prison guard would soon peak the interests of the other prisoners. For Ivan, he was still recovering back in the medical area of the prison. Ivan still had a raging headache from being knocked out by Daniel.

\#

Ivan's Headache

\#

Ivan knew he couldn't go back into the prison population with this headache happening.

\#

"Uh, my head" said Ivan as he felt the pain.

\#

"Don't get up" said Angelica.

#

The ghostly conscious of Angelica was hoping to try to deter Ivan from causing further trouble. She knew her real attorney self wouldn't be happy if she heard such commotion from him.

#

"You are ruining your chances at freedom" said Angelica.

#

Ivan sat back in his bed, he refused to listen to the ghostly conscious.

#

"Please listen to me" continued Angelica, "I am just warning you as your conscious you should realize what you are doing only hurts you."

#

Again there was no response from Ivan, he was still unhappy that he was knocked out in the first place.

#

"I just want to see my brother again and be with him" sighed Ivan.

#

"But your brother Viktor wouldn't approve of what you are doing in prison" continued Angelica.

#

No Viktor wouldn't approve if he saw the incidents for himself. Ivan sighed as he tried to get himself up but the pain was so much for him.

#

"Please don't try to get up" said Angelica, "rest."

#

Ivan sighed, what choices did he have?

#

Resting Ivan

#

Ivan decided he needed time to heal, so he decided to rest. He couldn't believe the sort of trouble he had gotten himself into. He did get the feeling there was something off with the new prison guard that came to Enrico's defense.

#

"Yes, just rest Ivan, you will need it" said Angelica.

#

The ghostly conscious continued to hover over Ivan doing her best to protect him. She could see the medics were also doing their best to make sure Ivan would feel better when he gets back into the prison population.

#

"I can't believe that Ivan found his match" whispered one of the medics as she was doing her chores.

#

"Yes, he is such a brute around the other prisoners he got what was coming to him" added another medic.

#

The women medics agreed that Ivan was a troublemaker in prison who finally was taught a valuable lesson. Ivan should have never lunged at his supporter Enrico Russo in that manner or be triggered by the new prison guard for just taking his tray to the kitchen counter. Everyone knew he had behavior issues, as the hours ticked by Ivan was feeling well enough to head back into the prison population.

#

Rejoining the Prison Population

#

Ivan soon found himself being escorted by prison guards once the medics determine he was okay to head back with the rest of the prison population.

#

"Uh, I do not think he should be allowed in" said one of the women medics to a prison guard.

#

"Rules are sadly rules" said the prison guard.

#

Ivan found himself in chains, as he was being escorted back to his cell the cells were all but empty. It was free time for the prison, and the prisoners got to do what they wanted.

#

"Lucky for you it's free time, no one is here to see your face" said another prison guard.

#

Daniel then noticed Ivan heading back in his cell, perfect timing thought Daniel. For Ivan, he noticed Daniel and soon felt frighten by his presence.

#

"Get me out of here!" cried Ivan.

#

The prison guards struggled trying to put him back in his cell.

#

"You have to go back first before we can release your chains" said one of the guards.

#

Ivan was clearly frighten by the new prison guard's presence, who could blame him. Daniel was brave enough to take a swipe at Ivan.

#

Releasing the Chains

#

The prison guards were able to get Ivan into his cell and unlock each of the chains. All Ivan wanted to do was make a mad dash to safety! He could see Daniel approaching calmly and cautiously towards his cell.

#

"I just wanted to speak to you" said Daniel.

#

"Please stay away from me!" cried Ivan.

#

Ivan was paranoid about the new prison guard, he bolted out after the last chains were released from him.

#

"Wow, he's fast!" laughed one of the prison guards.

#

Daniel knew work had to be done if he wanted to gain Ivan's trust. That incident at the mess hall didn't seem to help. Ivan darted around the many hallways of the prison. The other prisoners and staff alike backed away over his reputation.

#

"STAY AWAY FROM ME!" cried a white male prisoner.

#

"YEA, DO NOT COME CLOSE!" added a black gang member.

#

Ivan made another turn and soon came face to face with Yuri Kozlov. Yuri cracked his knuckles and soon moved towards Ivan.

#

"Well, well, well you finally snapped and poured boiling water on me" laughed Yuri, "but you also tried to attack one of your supporters from what I have heard from other prisoners."

#

Yuri had a crackle of a laugh that echoed throughout the hallways that sounded so sinister in its tone.

Chapter Five

Daniel Steps In

\#

The frightful return of Yuri soon brought the same fear again. However, Daniel Ward soon arrived. The former Major knew he had to separate the two prisoners fast! So he decided to step right in between.

\#

"ENOUGH, Ivan you do not want to get in any further trouble than you already have" said Daniel.

\#

"You must be the new prison guard that Enrico was speaking to the other day" said Yuri.

\#

"So what if I am, you and your men shouldn't be thinking about messing with me" said Daniel.

\#

"What are you going to do about it if we do?" laughed Yuri.

\#

Daniel didn't want to show off any of his MMA fighting skills at least not yet. Yuri on the other hand was about to throw a punch, that is until Daniel managed to grab his fist before it could ever reach him.

"Like I said, you do not want to interfere with me" said Daniel.

#

The grip by Daniel's grasp of Yuri's fist was so strong that Yuri couldn't even move.

#

"Hey, what gives?!" cried Yuri.

#

Yuri tried with all of his might, but Daniel had a calm demeanor in his manner.

#

<u>Calm Daniel</u>

#

Daniel continued to hold onto Yuri's fist preventing it from moving forward or being pulled away.

#

"What gives here?!" cried Yuri.

#

"I said please do not cause any further trouble this doesn't go for just Ivan but you as well and anyone else" said Daniel.

Daniel soon lets go of Yuri's fist and Yuri starts to stumble backwards nearly falling on the floor.

\#

"Uh, what are you!" cried Yuri.

\#

Yuri knew he had to have a better strategy than to just approach Ivan or this new guard. He had to sought out Tamrat and Emnet to implement their plan, now that Yuri knew what he was up against. He headed off trying to search for the two Ethiopian criminals, meanwhile for Ivan he was perplexed what just happened.

\#

"You shouldn't have fought your friend Enrico like that, he does miss trying to help you" said Daniel.

\#

"Who, who are you?" asked Ivan.

\#

Ivan was confused about how Daniel ended up as a prison guard. Little did he realize it was the help of Olga who created the fake job application from the prison system itself that got Daniel into the system.

\#

Protected by Daniel

#

Ivan strolled along the prison hallways with Daniel Ward. Daniel soon introduced Ivan as a former Major and MMA fighter. Ivan was impressed by Daniel's feet of skills.

#

"I can't believe you defended me" said Ivan, "after all what I have done in the past."

#

Ivan did felt guilt for what he had done back in the mess hall, trying to get into a fight with Daniel wasn't the wisest decision at all.

#

"Look, you need to be more careful" said Daniel.

#

Daniel soon mentioned he was hired by Boris Orlova to protect him while Ivan's attorney Angelica Esposito did her best trying to set him free.

#

"Your actions in prison only delay your prospects of freedom" said Daniel, "Boris wasn't happy with the incident with the boiling water."

Ivan lowered his head in shame, he couldn't believe he had overreacted like that. Pouring boiling water on Yuri, Tamrat and Emnet. Daniel thought of a possible strategy trying to cool down the tensions with the prisoners.

#

"Ivan, I want you to try to come up with an apology to the three prisoners" said Daniel.

#

"Me, apologizing, they were making fun of me" said Ivan.

#

"But two wrongs don't make a right" continued Daniel, "you know that.

#

Daniel knew he had his work cut out for him in terms of coaching Ivan to say an apology to the three prisoners.

#

Coaching Ivan

#

Daniel decided to keep a watchful eye on Ivan as Ivan was doing his chores around the prison. Enrico could see the difference in Ivan's behavior already.

#

"Hey, nice job in calming him down" said Enrico, "I know I couldn't go it myself."

#

"Well, since you were behind bars so long in the prison it made it harder for you to see it from another perspective" said Daniel.

#

"True, that's true" added Enrico.

#

Enrico nodded and went off on his way doing his own chores around the prison. For Yuri, the presence of Daniel Ward, a former Major and MMA fighter complicated matters. He already knew his name from his own loyalists in the prison and so did Tamrat and Emnet. The trio met in the yard in the prison.

#

"That new guard is going to be trouble for all three of us" said Yuri, "I couldn't lay one finger on him."

#

"Well from the reports from our allies" said Tamrat, "he threw a pretty good punch to Ivan."

#

"Yea, it was about time that fool got taught a lesson" laughed Emnet.

#

"There is the matter of using your associate Emnet for a distraction, we just need to figure out what it is" added Yuri.

#

"I know, you should get into a fight with another prisoner" laughed Tamrat, "that would force him to stop hovering over Ivan."

#

The trio agreed on implementing their little scheme so that they could get back at Ivan.

#

Emnet Starting a Fight

#

After the meeting between Yuri, Tamrat and Emnet, the lone Ethiopian criminal headed off throughout the prison trying to pick an easy fight. He soon noticed Daniel was too close to Ivan observing Ivan doing his cleaning chores.

#

"Nuts, I need to cause a distraction soon" said Emnet.

#

Emnet glanced around the hallways and noticed a few white and Hispanic prisoners were putting away supplies for the prison. He then noticed Yuri and Tamrat were just approaching Ivan down the hallway.

#

"Now is my chance" said Emnet.

#

Emnet wasn't a known troublemaker in the prison, but he was always determine to follow Tamrat's orders. The unlucky prisoners who were just putting away supplies were an easy target. The Ethiopian headed over towards where the group of prisoners were just putting away supplies and soon knocked them down with his own fist - WHAM! The supplies were sent tumbling down.

#

"Hey, why did you do that?!" cried one of the male prisoners.

#

"You'll see" laughed Emnet.

#

Emnet then surprised one of the other prisoners by knocking him out. Daniel saw the commotion and knew he had to break up the fight.

Chapter Six

Ivan Alone

\#

Ivan was finally alone to his own thoughts, but he didn't realize Emnet's little stunt with the other prisoners was a mere distraction. He didn't see the two shadows approach him from behind.

\#

"Ah yes, peace and quiet for Ivan" said Ivan.

\#

Before Ivan could realize it, Yuri grabbed him around the neck with his hands while Tamrat soon began to lift him up.

\#

"W-W-What are you doing?!" cried Ivan.

\#

The two prisoners were trying to abduct Ivan, trying to put him in another spot where Daniel wouldn't come to his rescue.

\#

"You have gone too far for what you have done to us!" laughed Yuri.

\#

"Yea, you messed with the bull, now you mess with its horns" laughed Tamrat.

#

Ivan tried to call for help, but there were no words that came out. For Daniel, breaking up the fight between Emnet and the other prisoners was an easy task. However it was long enough for Yuri and Tamrat to just abduct Ivan from behind.

#

"Alright, break it up" said Daniel.

#

The other prisoners backed away after seeing Daniel present. Emnet laughed as he noticed Ivan was missing.

#

"Looks like our plan worked!" laughed Emnet.

#

"What plan?!" cried Daniel.

#

Daniel gasped as he turned around, Ivan was missing!

#

Missing Ivan!

#

Daniel was in shock to find that Ivan Zhuk was gone! Just like that!

#

"YOU!" bellowed Daniel to Emnet, "What happened to him?!"

#

"Hey like I am going to talk to you, my job is done causing that little distraction" laughed Emnet.

#

Emnet was about to walk away when Daniel decided to take it up a notch. He lunged towards Emnet and began to tackle him.

#

"You will tell me what your friend is going to do with Ivan" said Daniel.

#

The other prisoners soon ran for their lives as they didn't want to get into Daniel's way.

#

"Alright, alright!" cried Emnet, "I was asked to cause a distraction for Tamrat and Yuri. They took Ivan!"

#

"WHERE?!" bellowed Daniel.

#

"I don't know, just around the prison!" cried Emnet.

#

Daniel dropped Emnet, he knew the Ethiopian was refusing to speak any further. He had to reach out to Enrico fast. He knew the prison's ins and outs. As he raced around the corner he soon spotted the Italian mobster doing some cleaning chores.

#

"Enrico, Ivan was abducted by Yuri and Tamrat" said Daniel, "I need your help to find him."

#

Enrico stopped what he was doing, he knew he had to help Daniel.

#

Worried for Ivan

#

Both Daniel and Enrico raced around the prison trying to figure out where Ivan had been taken to by Yuri and Tamrat. Emnet wasn't cooperating on what Yuri had planned to do, but then Daniel remembered about the shower incident earlier that Yuri took a terrible fall.

#

"The shower area" said Daniel, "I hope we're not too late."

#

Both Daniel and Enrico rushed over to the shower area, surely enough a row of black gang members and Yuri's own people stood in their path.

\#

"There is no way you will get through" said one of Yuri's henchmen.

\#

"What's going on with Ivan!" cried Enrico.

\#

"Boss is going to humiliate him like he did to himself the other day" added another Yuri henchman.

\#

Daniel knew he had to fight his way through the row of prisoners, as soon as Daniel began to get into his MMA fighting position, the other prisoners knew they had to make room.

\#

"Great, bosses are not going to like this" added a black gang member.

\#

Daniel and Enrico were not prepared to comprehend what Ivan was going through. Ivan found himself on the floor of the shower with Yuri delivering a few blows right and left.

\#

Paying Back for Humiliation

#

Yuri was having the time of his life punching poor Ivan. Ivan was helpless in this situation, even Tamrat joined in by pushing Ivan down.

#

"PLEASE STOP!" cried Ivan.

#

Tamrat then turned on the shower and the rush of water soon made it difficult for Ivan to stand up properly. He was getting all wet, but Yuri continued with the blows right and left - WHAM, WHAM, WHAM!

#

"THIS IS FOR MAKING ME FALL!" bellowed Yuri.

#

Yuri knew he had to be quick about this, he already could get the sense that the new prison guard was going to disrupt everything. Tamrat then joined in by kicking Ivan in the stomach.

#

"THIS IS FOR POURING BOILING WATER ON ME!" added Tamrat.

#

Ivan felt so much pain, he attempted to get up, but the water from the shower made everything slippery. He soon fell, Daniel pushed his way through the row of prisoners who were watching the fight. Then Daniel glanced at Yuri and Tamrat.

#

"YOU TWO!" bellowed Daniel.

#

Yuri was clearly frighten by Daniel's entrance, but Tamrat hadn't faced him before.

#

"He doesn't look tough" said Tamrat.

#

"Wait, don't!" cried Yuri.

#

It was too late, Tamrat charged at Daniel at full speed but instead Daniel managed to lift Tamrat up and did a body slam on him - WHAM!

Chapter Seven

Painful for Tamrat!

\#

The other prisoners were confused on what was happening, the black gang members saw their boss Tamrat injured on the ground.

\#

"YOU THREW OFF MY BACK!" cried Tamrat as he tried to get up.

\#

"You shouldn't have charged at me like that" said Daniel, "the rest of you, leave now!"

\#

Those were direct orders for the rest of the prisoners to disperse, the other prison guards soon came in with their riot gear. They had two injured prisoners - Ivan and Tamrat. Yuri would soon face solitary confinement for this little episode he brought upon Ivan.

\#

"Put him in solitary for abducting Ivan" said Daniel.

\#

"You're the boss" said one of the prison guards.

\#

Yuri soon found himself in handcuffs and soon hurled away. Ivan was once again put on a stretcher by the medics along with Tamrat. The medics sighed as they knew these were going to be the usual prisoners to take care of.

\#

"Not these two again" sighed one of the women medics.

\#

"Uh, tell me about it, can't believe they got into trouble again" added another woman medic.

\#

The women medics took Ivan and Tamrat back to the medical area of the prison.

\#

Daniel Thanks Enrico

\#

After Ivan and Tamrat were taken away again on stretchers, Daniel turned towards Enrico.

\#

"I am glad you knew where they were" said Daniel.

\#

"Hey, like I said, I know everything about this prison, its ins and its outs" continued Enrico, "Ivan is too stubborn to learn his lesson."

#

"He will have to, he needs to if he wants his freedom back" added Daniel, "I can't keep on doing this forever and neither can you."

#

"No, you're right, Ivan needs to be taught a lesson" added Enrico.

#

But Ivan was already learning a valuable lesson as he was taken away on a stretcher. He was still bruised up from the fight he had with Yuri in the shower with Tamrat. The conscious ghost of Ms. Angelica Esposito appeared before him.

#

"You realize your actions now have consequences in this prison?" asked Angelica.

#

All Ivan could do was nod his head, he was too weak to speak.

#

"Good, then you should get some rest, uh, can't believe you got yourself into trouble again" sighed Angelica.

#

The medics didn't see the conscious ghost of Angelica floating around as they brought both Ivan and Tamrat in.

#

Tamrat's Second Thoughts

#

Tamrat tried to pick himself up from the stretcher, but he was too weak. He couldn't believe that new guard had some fighting skills in him.

#

"Uh, who the heck was that guy!" cried Tamrat.

#

Tamrat couldn't really move, the medics did their best trying to provide some comfort.

#

"It looks like we might have to call an outside specialist for your injury" said one of the women medics.

#

"That's just terrific" sighed Tamrat in a sarcastic tone.

#

Tamrat wasn't happy the way things turned out to be. Yuri was still too much of a brute and knew this injury would force Tamrat to no longer have control of the prison. The truce was therefore off between him and the Russian mobster. He then glanced over to Ivan's area and noticed Ivan was glaring at someone that Tamrat couldn't see.

#

"What the hell are you looking at?" asked Tamrat.

#

Ivan glanced over, he was too weak to respond.

#

"My conscious" replied Ivan.

#

That spooked Tamrat, Ivan had identified the ghost of his conscious doing her best trying to try to help him in this time of crisis.

#

Reporting to Boris

#

While Tamrat and Ivan were resting in the medical area, Daniel had to report to Boris Orlova. During his break, he soon managed to call Boris on his cellphone.

#

"Daniel, what is there to report about Ivan's manners?" asked Boris.

#

"Things have taken a turn for the worse, Ivan doesn't seem to be improving that much" sighed Daniel.

#

"Really?" asked Boris, "What did he do this time?"

#

"He tried to get into a fight with Enrico Russo an Italian mobster for just coming to my defense" continued Daniel, "I knocked him out with one punch."

#

"Dear me" sighed Boris, "what other sort of progress have you made?"

#

"Well, I reminded Ivan that his behavior is sabotaging his efforts in gaining his freedom back" continued Daniel, "Enrico knows this as well."

#

"Yes, I spoke with him before I hired you in person" said Boris, "Ivan's behavior needs to improve if a judge wants to release him even under house arrest to my property."

#

"Yes, that's probably the likely scenario he'll end up in if he behaves" said Daniel, "I will try to also get him to apologize to the other prisoners for the boiling water incident."

#

"That will be a tough sell for him" added Boris, "best of luck."

#

As the phone conversation ended, Daniel had only hope that the attorney Ms. Angelica Esposito could change Ivan's mind.

Part Three

Chapter Eight

Upset Attorney

#

For the real Madame Angelica Esposito, Esq., she knew that Ivan Zhuk was a tough cookie to crack. It would take so much of an effort on Daniel's part to get Ivan to change his behavior while he works as a prison guard. She was having a Zoom meeting with Boris Orlova but also Congressman Zach Washington since he was also trying to get Yuri free.

#

"Congressman Washington, thank you for attending this meeting with Boris Orlova" said Angelica.

#

"Pleasure to be here" said Zach.

#

Congressman Zach Washington and his Blue Checker Party had everything to gain for a possible prisoner swap. It would make things less tense in the prison if Yuri Kozlov would be free in a prisoner exchange.

#

"So what is the time table for the prisoner exchange to happen?" asked Boris.

#

"That's sadly classified information coming from the Select Committee in Congress and the Senate" continued Zach, "things are moving at a snail's pace."

#

"At this rate, Ivan will sadly set the world record in creating more problems for that particular prison" sighed Boris.

#

"I know this seems a rather depressing time for you to see your client Ivan Zhuk behave like this" added Angelica.

#

"Yes" said Boris, "it's very clear Ivan will always be a troublemaker."

#

Suggestions from Angelica

#

Angelica brought up some sort of suggestions that she will issue the judge when they'll appear in court later in the month.

#

"Here is a list of suggestions I have for the judge when we appear in court on Ivan's behavior" continued Angelica, "Ivan will have an ankle bracelet on. He cannot leave Boris' premise at all."

#

"Fair enough, anything else?" asked Boris.

#

"An on site therapist that Ivan will have to regularly report to" continued Angelica, "regularly showing up to court on days he has to report in."

#

"My, my" said Boris.

#

"He will also have to be disciplined whenever he steps out of line" continued Angelica.

#

"Well, there is that former Major operating within the prison as a prison guard" said Boris, "maybe when Ivan gets to be released we can work something out."

#

"Yes, disciplining Ivan Zhuk is essential" continued Angelica, "he can be rather of a hassle."

#

For Congressman Zach Washington and his Blue Checker Party, he knew things would be rough so long as Yuri were still present.

#

"I will end this call seeing if I can get the Select Committee to move forward" said Zach.

#

"Yes, please do" added Angelica.

#

As the Zoom meeting ended, Boris had only hope that Ivan didn't get himself into further trouble.

#

Yuri Leaves Solitary

#

Yuri Kozlov's time in solitary confinement was over, the prison guards soon escorted him out of the cell and soon escorted him back towards his original cell. He gazed over the many cells that were filled up with other prisoners before him. His own men welcomed him back.

#

"Nice to see you out of solitary again boss" said one of the henchmen.

#

"Yes, nice job in going after Ivan" added another henchman.

#

It was like that, Yuri had regained control over the prison with the grasp against Ivan Zhuk. And also got his main rival - Tamrat Hailu injured in the process. Tamrat was too overconfident to go after the new prison guard and Yuri knew it.

\#

"Ha, that Ethiopian was a fool going after the new guard" laughed Yuri.

\#

But Yuri soon had to shut his own trap as he noticed Daniel Ward in his prison guard uniform.

\#

"So you're out from solitary" said Daniel, "you better not cause anymore trouble. I am keeping an eye on you."

\#

"And you better stop protecting that Ivan he is bad news" added Yuri.

\#

Yuri soon is escorted to his main cell, where the prisoners were told to have lights out.

\#

Checking Up on Ivan

\#

As the prisoners soon fell asleep, Daniel decided to stroll to the medical area of the prison. He could see there were plenty of other prisoners who had injuries, but he was trying to find out where Ivan was located.

#

"Ivan Zhuk, he's just a few paces down that way" said a woman medic.

#

"Thank you" said Daniel.

#

Daniel headed off towards the direction, as he approached the corner around the hallway he noticed the number associated with Ivan's bed. He headed over to the room where Ivan was resting.

#

"Ivan, are you okay?" asked Daniel.

#

Ivan looked up, he couldn't believe that Daniel still had high hopes for him.

#

"Why are you still believing in someone like me?" asked Ivan.

#

"I believe there is always good in all of us" added Daniel.

#

Ivan coughed a bit.

\#

"Uh, still can't believe Yuri tricked you like that with that other Ethiopian" sighed Ivan.

\#

"Well, it seems Tamrat might be lurking around in another room" said Daniel.

\#

"Please stay with me, I don't want to be alone" said Ivan.

\#

Daniel could see how fearful Ivan was becoming, the mental breakdown of being in prison was getting to him.

Chapter Nine

<u>Staying with Ivan</u>

#

Daniel stayed for longer than anticipated by Ivan's side, this was the perfect time for Daniel to try to teach Ivan to apologize to the other prisoners for what he had done to them. Daniel grabbed a notepad with a pen.

#

"Ivan, I think it's time you ought to write an apology letter to Tamrat, Emnet and Yuri for pouring boiling water on them" said Daniel, "it would ease off the tensions with all of you."

#

Ivan thought of it, words couldn't come to Ivan's mind on what to write.

#

"But, what if they do not accept it?" asked Ivan.

#

"Even someone like Yuri could understand what an apology is" said Daniel, "even he would appreciate it as much as Tamrat and Enmet."

#

Ivan held his breath.

#

"Give me the pen and notepad" said Ivan.

#

Ivan did his best trying to write his apology letter to Tamrat. He was going to address them separately. He had to think of what to say with each letter that he wrote. With Tamrat, he wanted to apologize for not helping him when he was welcomed into his inner circle. Emnet had to be a separate letter.

#

The Apology Letters

#

Daniel began to read the first letter to Tamrat, lucky for Ivan, Tamrat was just a few paces down trying to recover from the back injury when Tamrat tried to lunge at Daniel.

#

"Yes, this looks perfect" said Daniel as he skimmed the letter.

#

The letter was from Ivan's heart, he couldn't believe what a terrible person he was towards Tamrat. Daniel held his breath and headed down the hallway towards Tamrat's bed.

#

"It's you" sighed Tamrat, "what do you want."

#

"Ivan wrote you an apology letter" said Daniel, "and foremost I apologize for breaking your back like that. You know, you should have listened to Yuri."

#

"Yea, yea, just give me the letter" said Tamrat.

#

Daniel hands Tamrat the letter, much to Tamrat's surprise, Tamrat couldn't believe how emotional Ivan was. He burst out with laughter, but this was a nice brand of laughter, not mocking Ivan in any fashion.

#

"Well I be, he really is sorry for pouring the boiling water on me" said Tamrat.

#

"So will you make things easy on him when you do recover?" asked Daniel.

#

"I would still have to think about it" said Tamrat, "Ivan has ruined his reputation too much around the prison. You understand."

#

Daniel sighed as he headed back to Ivan's bed.

Daniel's Input

#

Daniel strolled right back towards Ivan's bed, Ivan glanced over and noticed Daniel.

#

"Well, what did he have to say?" asked Ivan.

#

"He said he'd think about it" said Daniel, "you have caused so much trouble in this prison."

#

"I know" sighed Ivan, "I am very sorry for it."

#

"The other letters, let me see them" said Daniel.

#

Daniel looked over the letter to Emnet. A smile grew on Daniel's face and then the letter to Yuri.

#

"I do not know if Yuri will lay off on you or the two Ethiopians" said Daniel, "but one thing is for sure, they will still be happy anyway you took in the effort in writing the letters. I will make sure to have a good word in for Boris about this."

\#

"Please do, I am sorry for the trouble I have caused him" added Ivan.

\#

Daniel headed off back to his patrol, he decided to stroll about towards the hallways where the prisoners were doing their chores. He noticed Emnet was now putting away supplies as punishment for disrupting the chores of other prisoners. Emnet soon froze as he noticed Daniel, frighten that Daniel might want some payback.

\#

The Letter to Emnet

\#

Emnet was no doubt frighten by Daniel's sudden appearance as the prison guard before him. He knew he didn't do anything wrong this time.

\#

"Please, it was a mistake for what I have done to Ivan" said Emnet.

\#

"Relax, I am just here to deliver you a letter he wrote to you" said Daniel.

\#

Emnet was shocked, a letter for him? Emnet was handed over the letter. It took some time for Emnet to read and skim the letter. Just like Tamrat, he let out a happy crackle of a laugh. No one has ever written Emnet a letter before in his entire life, not even an apology letter!

\#

"Wow, Ivan really does want to change!" laughed Emnet.

\#

"Yep, I hope you can give him that chance" continued Daniel, "no more prison power struggles in using him as a pawn."

\#

"No sir, we will do our best to help Ivan once he fully recovers" laughed Emnet.

\#

"Good, tell your boss to make sure that'd be his motto once he recovers" added Daniel.

\#

Daniel was pleased that Emnet was happy with the apology letter. He didn't know if Yuri would feel the same.

Chapter Ten

<u>Finding Yuri</u>

\#

Daniel continued to stroll through the hallways trying his best to find Yuri Kozlov. He knew the Russian mobster couldn't have gotten that far. Then he knew where to look for him - the prison's exercise area. Yuri was pumping some weights when Daniel soon showed up.

\#

"You again, here to bother me, mock my skills?" asked Yuri.

\#

"Actually no, Ivan who is recovering in the medical area wrote you an apology letter for pouring the boiling water on him" said Daniel.

\#

Daniel soon hands Yuri the letter. The Russian mobster soon skims it. However, the letter didn't seem to change Yuri's mind at all.

\#

"YOU think just one letter will change my mind about that MAN?!" bellowed Yuri.

\#

Yuri knew it wasn't wise to pick a fight with an MMA fighter, especially one that didn't allow him to lay a finger on him.

"So it seems that a letter won't change your behavior" sighed Daniel, "I guess I will have to protect Ivan until the judge gets him out."

#

"Ha, fat chance, I will make sure that Ivan will always get into solitary confinement, if I am not the one causing the problem, there will be others who will!" laughed Yuri.

#

The letter didn't move Yuri unlike Tamrat and Emnet. He was dead set on hating Ivan for what he did with the boiling water and for the fact he was a Ukrainian.

#

Typical Yuri

#

Daniel could have felt that Yuri wouldn't be moved by such an apology letter. He glanced over as Yuri continued his exercises lifting weights.

#

"Sigh, there is nothing that'd change that man's mind about Ivan" thought Daniel in his own head.

#

Daniel headed off down the hallway, he soon passed Enrico who was doing some cleaning chores around the prison.

#

"So I take you spoke with Ivan, how is he feeling?" asked Enrico.

#

"He's feeling better, he will likely be back in the prison population before Tamrat would" continued Daniel, "he also wrote Yuri, Tamrat and Emnet apology letters."

#

Enrico paused for a moment. This was certainly out of character of Ivan's own behavior.

#

"I spoke to him about his behavior sabotaging his freedom efforts" added Daniel.

#

"Yes" said Enrico, "it is really a self-defeating behavior."

#

"Tamrat and Emnet seem like they're leaning to leave Ivan alone but not Yuri" said Daniel.

#

"That's just typical of him, he will never change he is always out against anyone who is Ukrainian" said Enrico.

#

"Yes, I suppose a letter from one of them or all of them wouldn't dare change his mind" added Daniel, "but that's life can't change everyone."

\#

Daniel continued to stroll off, once he got into the staff lounge he soon decided to report this to Boris.

\#

Reporting on the Apology Letters

\#

Daniel soon began to call Boris, Boris soon was able to pick up. He was busy in his office trying to look at the calendar for the court date for Ivan's case.

\#

"Daniel, what have you to report to me?" asked Boris.

\#

"Ivan's behavior is improving, he wrote three apology letters to Yuri, Tamrat and Emnet" continued Daniel.

\#

"You got him to write apology letters for the boiling water incident?" asked Boris.

\#

Boris was shocked by this development, this would be good news for Angelica to hear.

#

"Tamrat and Emnet are leaning to leave Ivan alone, but not Yuri" continued Daniel, "that man has issues."

#

"I can imagine, being a mobster loyal to the Russian government is something that we cannot get around" said Boris, "he will always be loyal to the Kremlin."

#

"Yes, that's the sad care for Yuri, but I hope you are also working through channels on getting Yuri out first" added Daniel.

#

"I am in contact with Congressman Zach Washington of the Blue Checker Party, their party has shifted towards being against the Kremlin since the last few election cycles" continued Boris.

#

"Good, see if they can speed things up" added Daniel.

#

After the phone conversation with Boris, Daniel continued on his patrol.

#

Letting Angelica Know

\#

Boris knew he had to call Ivan's attorney - Madame Angelica Esposito Esq.! As he did, she quickly answered the phone.

\#

"Boris, didn't expect you to be so quick after the Zoom meeting" said Angelica.

\#

"Well, I have good news, your client Ivan has sent three apology letters to Yuri, Tamrat and Emnet!" laughed Boris.

\#

"That's wonderful news, did any of them accept the apology?" asked Angelica.

\#

"From Daniel's point, only Tamrat and Emnet were intrigued and moved by the apology letter" continued Boris, "but not Yuri. Yuri still doesn't like anyone who is Ukrainian."

\#

"Dear me, maybe having them appear before a judge will get to change Yuri's mind if Yuri wants to leave the prison back to his home country of Russia" continued Angelica.

\#

"Yes, that will be a wise decision, especially for Yuri's safety and Ivan's" continued Boris, "anyway I hope to see you at the court."

#

"Yes, will do" laughed Angelica.

#

Angelica Esposito was so excited over hearing that Ivan was changing his tune. She had high hopes that his behavior would only improve and get better instead of dragging it out. They would all have to wait until the court day would happen.

Epilogue

Ivan Heads Back

\#

Much like Daniel's speculation, Ivan was released from the medical area of the prison first before Tamrat. A specialized doctor was called to the medical area to inspect Tamrat's injuries while Ivan got to go free.

\#

"So I hope you will cause no further trouble" said one of the prison guards as they continued to escort Ivan back to the main prison area.

\#

The other prisoners who heard of the apology letters that Ivan wrote had a different take on him. They were no longer frighten by Ivan's appearance as he was being escorted back to his cell.

\#

"Hey, that was some letter you wrote for Tamrat" said a black gang member.

\#

"Yea, it takes real guts to write something like that" added a Hispanic male prisoner.

\#

It was much of the same attitude, until Ivan soon was approaching Yuri's cell.

\#

"I did receive your little letter and no I am not going to change my mind about you" laughed Yuri, "you think one letter changes someone's mind? It doesn't!"

\#

Yuri was defiant as the prison guards continued to escort Ivan back to his cell. Ivan was pleased the other prisoners soon began to respect him more.

\#

Daniel's Lesson

\#

Daniel Ward awaited Ivan near his cell as Ivan was escorted inside. The prison guards soon took off the chains and allowed him to be free in his cell.

\#

"So, I take you learned a valuable lesson in apologizing to those around you?" asked Daniel.

\#

Ivan nodded.

\#

"Yes, but when will I get to have my freedom again?" asked Ivan.

\#

"Patience, I am in contact with Boris, he states the court date will be at the end of the month" continued Daniel, "just keep up the good behavior and maybe, just maybe you'll be released."

\#

Ivan felt rather confident that he would soon be freed. There was still the matter of facing off with Yuri. Yuri was unmoved by the apology letter, but the rest of the prison all felt a different tone. No longer would they fear Ivan at all but instead welcome him. Even Enrico welcomed Ivan's return.

\#

"Those were some tear jerking letters you wrote" laughed Enrico.

\#

"I am sorry for lunging at you" said Ivan.

\#

"Yea, I accept your apology" said Enrico, "but please do not be so rash the next time. Think ahead first."

\#

Enrico also had a few points to Ivan as they were in their cells.

\#

Tamrat Recovers

\#

Time soon passed and Daniel Ward would always be the one to watch over Ivan Zhuk, protecting him at every turn with the assistance of Enrico Russo. Together they would be determine to help Ivan out. Emnet who didn't have that much control over the black gangs lacked the charisma to help. Though they respected Ivan's bravery in writing the apology letters the orders needed to come from the top - coming from Tamrat himself. Soon the day came and Tamrat was released from the medical area. He was escorted back towards his cell by the prison guards.

\#

"Uh, so glad to be out of the medical area, I will never try to fight an MMA fighter ever again" sighed Tamrat.

\#

Tamrat could see the change in the mood of the other prisoners when it came to Ivan's own name. The apology letters had an impact on the prison population. All they had to do was say they were sorry for their crimes like how Ivan did. As for Ivan's freedom, would Ivan Zhuk gain his freedom? Would Yuri get even again or go back to Russia? Find out in the next exciting book!

* * *

Don't miss out!

Visit the website below and you can sign up to receive emails whenever Maxwell Hoffman publishes a new book. There's no charge and no obligation.

https://books2read.com/r/B-A-JVYOC-EHGDF

BOOKS 2 READ

Connecting independent readers to independent writers.

About the Author

I graduated from California State University with a BA in History. I am fond of historical fiction, science fiction, fantasy, and horror.

Read more at https://www.instagram.com/vader7800/.

About the Publisher

I graduated from California State University of Northridge with a BA in History. I am fond of fantasy, science fiction, historical fiction and horror.

Read more at https://www.instagram.com/vader7800/.

Milton Keynes UK
Ingram Content Group UK Ltd.
UKHW042002281024
450365UK00003B/90